Hurry, Santa!

For Eleanor Troth &
Emily Peopall
~ *J.S.*

For Jane,
who *loves* Christmas!
~ *T.W.*

ISBN 0-439-08372-9

Text copyright © 1998 by Julie Sykes.
Illustrations copyright © 1998 by Tim Warnes.
All rights reserved. Published by Scholastic Inc., 555 Broadway, New York, NY
10012, by arrangement with Little Tiger Press, an imprint of Magi Publications.

12 11 10 9 8 7 6 5 4 3 2 1   9/9 0 1 2 3 4/0

Printed in the U.S.A.   08

First Scholastic printing, November 1999

Hurry, Santa!

by Julie Sykes

Pictures by Tim Warnes

SCHOLASTIC INC.
New York Toronto London Auckland Sydney
Mexico City New Delhi Hong Kong

It was Christmas Eve, Santa's busiest time of year. But Santa was fast asleep, snoring under his blanket.

"Wake up!" squeaked Santa's little mouse, tugging at his beard. "Hurry, Santa! You can't be late tonight."

"Ouch!" cried Santa, sitting up and rubbing his chin. "Goodness, is that clock right? The alarm didn't go off, and I've overslept."

Santa leapt out of bed and began to pull
on his clothes. He was in such a hurry that
he put both feet in one pant leg and fell flat
on his face.

"Hurry, Santa!" meowed the cat. "You can't be late tonight."

"No, I can't," agreed Santa, getting back up. "I can't be late delivering the presents."

When he was finally dressed, Santa hurried
outside to his sleigh. He picked up the harness
and tried to put it on the reindeer.

But the reindeer weren't there!

"Oh no!" cried Santa. "Where can they be?"

"The reindeer are loose in the woods," called Fox.
"You'd better catch them before they wander off.
Hurry, Santa, you can't be late tonight."
"No, I can't," agreed Santa, running toward the trees.

Deep in the woods some
of the reindeer were having a
snowball fight.

"Aaaaah!" shouted Santa as
a snowball hit him in the face.

"Hurry, Santa," hooted Owl. "You don't have time to play in the snow."

"But I wasn't playing!" said Santa.

He searched all over for the other reindeer, but they were nowhere to be found. "I hope you four can pull the sleigh by yourselves," he said. "Come on, we've got work to do."

At last Santa took off, steering
the sleigh toward the moon.
"Go, Reindeer, go!" he shouted.
"We can't be late tonight!"

Around the world they flew, delivering their presents.

"Down again," called Santa, turning the sleigh toward a farm.

"Hurry, Santa!" answered the reindeer. "We're miles from anywhere, and the night's almost over."

"I'm doing my best," boomed Santa, flicking the reins.

Before he knew what was happening,
the reindeer quickened their pace.
  "Whoa," Santa cried, but it was too late.
Landing with a bump, the sleigh skidded
crazily across the snow.
  "Oooooh deeeaaar!" cried Santa.

CRASH!

The sleigh had gotten stuck in a giant snowdrift. Santa scrambled to his feet and rubbed his bruised bottom. "Nothing broken," he said. "But we must hurry!"

When the reindeer had untangled themselves,
they tried to dig out the sleigh. They tugged and
pulled and pushed as hard as they could, but the
sleigh was completely stuck in the snow.

"It's no use," wailed the reindeer. "We can't move this sleigh on our own."

"We must keep trying," said Santa. "The sky is getting lighter, and we're running out of time."

Suddenly Santa heard a loud neigh. Trotting toward them was a very large horse.

"Hurry, Santa!" she neighed. "You've still got presents to deliver. *I'll* help you move your sleigh."

So they all pulled together, even Santa's little mouse, but it was no good. The sleigh was still stuck.

"Hurry, Santa!" called the rooster from the barnyard.
"It's nearly morning."

"I am *trying* to hurry," puffed Santa. "One more pull,
everyone!"

At last the sleigh began to move. . . .

And Santa tumbled backward, cheering
loudly.

"Hurry, Santa!" called all the animals.
"The sun's rising. You've got to finish your
rounds before the children wake up."

"Yes," agreed Santa. "It's nearly
Christmas Day!"

It was a close call, but by dawn Santa had managed
to deliver every present. Finally, he and the reindeer
arrived back at the North Pole.

"We did it!" yawned Santa. "I wasn't—"

He stopped talking and stared at his sack in dismay. At the very bottom was a present.

"Oh no, how awful!" he cried. "I've forgotten someone!"

Then Santa saw that all the animals were
laughing at him.

"That present is for *you*," said the reindeer.
"It's from all of us."

"Hurry, Santa!" added the little mouse. "You should open your present. It's Christmas Day!"

"Yes, I should," chuckled Santa. "Now, I wonder what it is. . . ."